A Visit to
JAPAN

Peter & Connie Roop

Heinemann Library
Des Plaines, Illinois

Designed by AMR
Illustrations by Art Construction
Printed in Hong Kong / China

02 01 00 99
10 9 8 7 6 5 4 3 2 1

Library of Congress Cataloging-in-Publication Data

Roop, Peter.
      Japan / Peter & Connie Roop.
         p.   cm. -- (Visit to)
      Includes index.
      Summary: Introduces the country of Japan, including the land,
landmarks, homes, food, clothes, work, transportation, language,
school, sports, celebrations, and the arts.
      ISBN 1-57572-712-9
      1. Japan--Pictorial works--juvenile literature.   [1. Japan.]
I. Roop, Connie.   II. Series: Roop, Peter. Visit to.
DS806.R56   1998
952--dc21   98-12448
                                                                                           CIP
                                                                                            AC

Acknowledgements
The Publishers would like to thank the following for permission to reproduce photographs:
J. Allan Cash: pp. 9, 12, 16, 18; Colorific!: de Marcillac p. 28; B. Glinn-Magnum p. 20; Hutchison Library: J. Burbank pp. 5, 22, 24, 29, R. Francis p. 23, M. Harvey pp. 10, 11, M. MacIntyre p. 13; Images Color Library: pp. 8, 14, 15, 21, 25; JNTO: p.26; Panos Pictures: J. Holmes pp. 6, 7, 19; Trip: C. McCooey p. 27

Cover photograph reproduced with permission of P. Rauter, Trip

Every effort has been made to contact copyright holders of any material reproduced in this book. Any omissions will be rectified in subsequent printings if notice is given to the Publisher.

 Any words appearing in bold, **like this**, are explained in the Glossary.

Contents

Japan

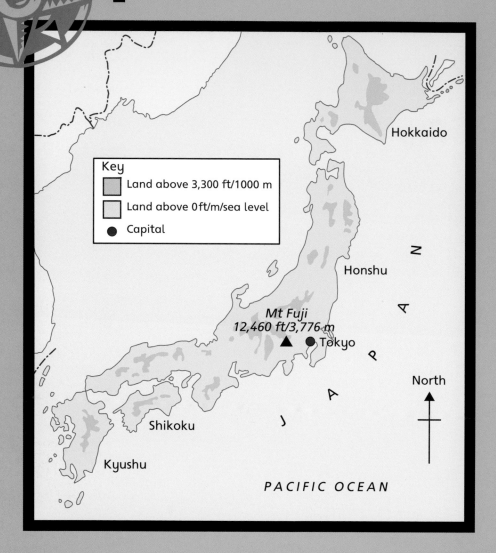

Key
- Land above 3,300 ft/1000 m
- Land above 0 ft/m/sea level
- ● Capital

Hokkaido

Honshu

Mt Fuji
12,460 ft/3,776 m ▲ ● Tokyo

JAPAN

North

Shikoku

Kyushu

PACIFIC OCEAN

Japan is an island country in Asia. There are 4,000 islands in Japan. Most people live on the four biggest islands.

The building in this picture is on the island of Honshu. Japanese eat, sleep, go to school, and play like you. Life in Japan is also **unique**.

Land

Japan has many mountains and **volcanoes.**
Some of the volcanoes **erupt.** Japan has
about 1,500 **earthquakes** each year.

Japan is a very long country. The islands in the north can have snow while the islands in the south are still warm. All of the islands have **typhoons**.

Landmarks

Mount Fuji is Japan's most famous mountain. Mount Fuji is a **volcano**. It has not **erupted** for hundreds of years.

Tokyo is the **capital** of Japan. Tokyo is Japan's largest city. One out of every ten Japanese lives in Tokyo.

Homes

Most Japanese live in small buildings in crowded cities. Most of Japan's cities are on the lowlands near the coast.

In the country, the homes are made of wood. They are only one or two stories high. The Japanese always take their shoes off before entering a home.

Food

The Japanese enjoy making their food look attractive. They eat small portions of many different kinds of food, but noodles are a favorite food.

At home, the Japanese sit on the floor and eat from low, wooden tables. The Japanese use **chopsticks** to eat their food. Rice and hot tea are served at every meal.

Clothes

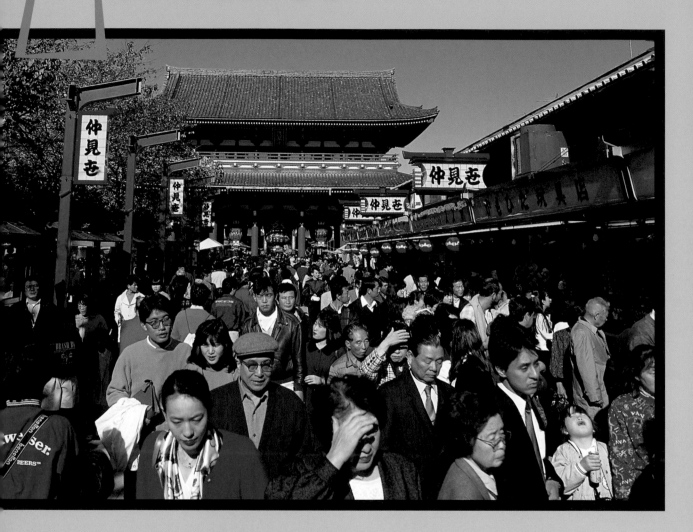

Most Japanese wear clothes like yours,
but they wear kimonos on special days.
Farmers wear **traditional** work clothes,
like baggy pants and straw hats.

A kimono is a long silk robe that is tied with a large sash. There is a different kimono for each season. The light, summer kimonos are called *yukata*.

Work

Only a few Japanese are farmers, but they grow most of Japan's food. They grow rice, wheat, soybeans, tea, fruit, and vegetables. They also keep pigs and chickens.

Japan's fishermen are very successful.
Only China's fishermen catch more
fish in one year. Most people in Japan
work in offices or **factories.**

Transportation

The bullet train is the fastest way to travel on land. It is a high speed train. Two of the islands are connected by the world's longest train tunnel.

Many people travel to work by train or
subway. Passengers are pushed onto
the trains by station workers! Airports
and roads link all the main cities.

Language

When Japanese people greet each other, they bow to show **respect**. They are very polite to each other.

It takes a long time to learn how to read and write Japanese. There are 1,850 **characters,** which are written in columns from right to left.

School

Children go to school from ages six to fifteen. They learn Japanese, math, English, physical education, and art. They also practice **earthquake drills**.

Even the young students study very hard. Each night they do hours of homework. Students work hard to get into a good college.

Free Time

Japan's national sport is sumo wrestling. Each wrestler has to throw the other one out of the ring. Millions of Japanese also enjoy baseball.

Many Japanese spend time in parks and gardens. A favorite time to visit is in the spring when the cherry trees are in blossom.

Celebrations

Japan has many festivals, but New Year is the biggest. The festival is like a giant birthday party. Everyone adds another year to their age!

Children's Day is celebrated on May 5.
Every family flies a **carp** kite or a
windsock for each child.

The Arts

The Japanese have many **traditional crafts.** They enjoy ink painting, flower arranging, and making beautiful pottery and origami. Origami is the art of folding paper.

Noh (NO) theater is only found in Japan. Actors wear masks to perform **ancient** stories. Musicians **accompany** them. They are also on stage and in costume.

Fact File

Name	Japan is the island country's full name.
Capital	The **capital** of Japan is Tokyo.
Languages	Most Japanese speak and write Japanese, but some can also speak Korean or English.
Population	There are about 125 million people living in Japan.
Money	Instead of the dollar, the Japanese have the yen.
Religions	Most Japanese believe in Buddhism and Shintoism. There are also some Christians.
Products	Japan produces rice, fish, steel, cameras, televisions, radios, ships, cars, chemicals, and toys.

Words You Can Learn

ee-chee (ee-tchee)	one
nee (nee)	two
sahn (san)	three
konnichi wa (kon-nee-tchee wa)	hello
sayonara (sah-yoh-nah-rah)	goodbye
arigato (aree-gah-toh)	thank you
hai (hi)	yes
iie (ee-eh)	no
okaasan (oh-kah-san)	respected mother
otoosan (oh-taw-san)	respected father

Glossary

accompany	to play an instrument while someone sings or speaks
ancient	from a long time ago
capital	the city where the government is based
carp	a kind of fish like a large goldfish
characters	the symbols or letters of an alphabet
chopsticks	a pair of sticks held in one hand to lift food to the mouth
crafts	nice things that are made by hand
drills	a safety exercise where people practice what to do when there is an emergency, like a fire or an earthquake
earthquake	violent shaking of the ground
erupt	throw out ash and melted rock
factories	places where many of the same things are made
respect	to think highly of someone
subway	trains that run underground through tunnels
traditional	the way things have been done or made for a long time
typhoons	big storms with strong winds and heavy rain
unique	different in a special way
volcano	a mountain or hole in the ground that sometimes throws out ash or melted rock from beneath the Earth's surface
windsock	a piece of cloth that blows in the wind

Index

More Books to Read

Bornoff, Nick. *Japan*. Chatham, NJ: Raintree Steck-Vaughn. 1997

Dahl, Michael. *Japan*. Danbury, CT: Children's Press. 1997.

Henrichs, Ann. *Japan*. Danbury, CT: Children's Press. 1997.

Pluckrose, Henry A. *Japan*. New York: Franklin Watts, Inc. 1998.